MY CASTLE

by Florence Parry Heide

drawings by Symeon Shimin

McGRAW-HILL BOOK COMPANY
New York · St. Louis · San Francisco · Düsseldorf · Johannesburg
Kuala Lumpur · London · Mexico · Montreal · New Delhi · Panama
Rio de Janeiro · Singapore · Sydney · Toronto

I live in a castle.
All summer long
I live in a castle.
I can see everything
from my castle.

I get awake

early in the morning.

I get awake, and

I can feel the wet dew on me

and on my pillow.

I cannot see the sun,

but I know the sun is coming.

I know the sun is coming

because all the lights on the street

are turned off,

all the music has stopped,

all the loud talking,

all the slamming,

all the laughing has stopped,

and it is quiet in the street.

I know the sun is coming

because the sky is getting pale and paler.

I have the best castle on the street

because it is the highest one.

Under my castle is the castle of my friends
Mr. and Mrs. Rodriguez.
They are still sleeping when I am first awake.

I am always the first one awake.
I can lie on my back and look at the sky.
I can turn on my stomach
and look at Mr. and Mrs. Rodriquez
still sleeping.

I can look down to the sidewalk.
I can look across the street
and see the stores and the taverns.
I can see all the doors and all the windows.

If I lean over,
I can see all the way up and down the street.

I can wait for the street to get awake.

Last night my mother gave me an apple
to save for the morning.

Now I can eat it.

After I eat the apple,
I pick out the little seeds.

I put the seeds in my box.

I have many seeds.
When I have a place to plant them,
I will plant them.

I wait to see what it is that is going to start the day.

Sometimes the day starts
with a truck coming down the street.

It is not always the same truck,
but the day almost always starts
with a truck coming.

Sometimes—

once in a while—

it starts with a dog walking down the street.

Sometimes it starts

with Mr. Yanowicz coming outside and stretching.

After the first thing happens,

lots of other things happen.

Mr. and Mrs. Rodriguez

go inside with their bed and their pillows.

A policeman walks down the street.

He does not see me.

Mr. Hannora opens the door of his store

and looks up and down the street.

He waves at me, I wave at him.

He does not know my name.

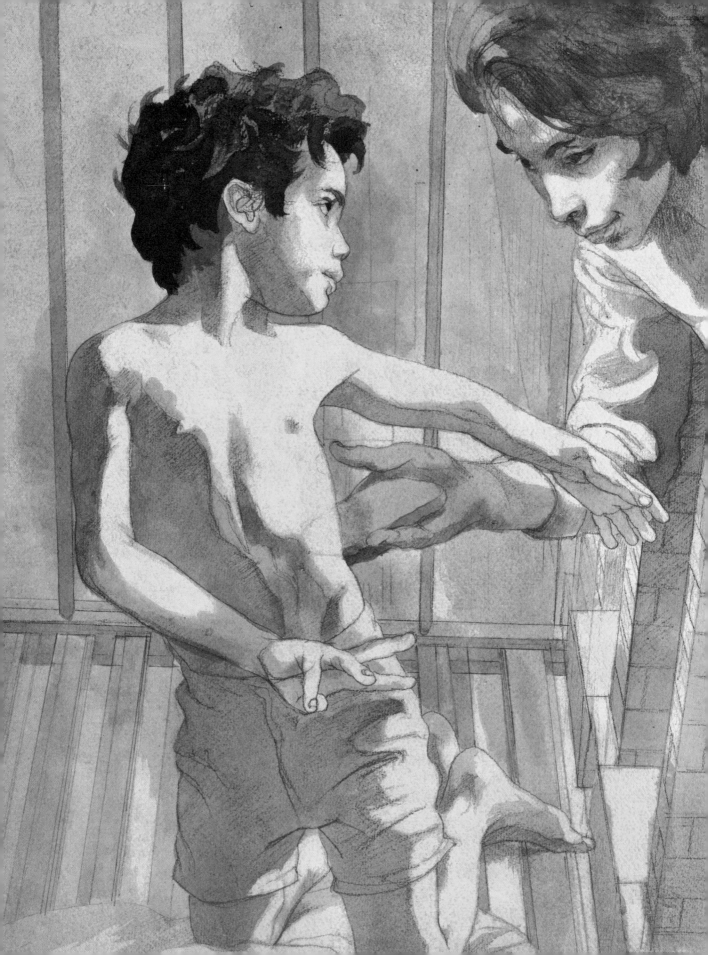

Soon other trucks come.

Other people are on the street.

Some of them are going to work.

They carry paper bags filled with sandwiches.

I watch and I listen.

I lie on my back

and watch the sky turn blue.

The day is bright now.

But I cannot see the sun

because it is behind the building across the street.

I like to stay out in my castle.

My mother hands me my bread and jelly

through the window.

"Be good," she says. "Don't go off the street

while I'm gone."

I eat my bread and jelly

while I watch her go down the street.

She waves good-by.

Nearly every day

something comes to my castle that is nice.

Sometimes

it is a little piece of paper

that blows to me from the street.

I smooth it out

and save it in my box.

Sometimes

it is a little spider that comes

to my castle.

I can watch it spinning its web

between the railings.

Once
there was a blue butterfly.
It only stayed for a minute
in my castle.

Then,
I think,
it flew off to tell the other butterflies
to come to see my castle.

I waited and waited,
but no butterflies came.

Sometimes
a leaf blows into my castle.

I try to smooth it out,
but it soon cracks in pieces.

I save the little pieces in my box.

I think it is going to rain.

Mother said
if it rained, I must cover my castle
to keep it dry.

I climb in through the window
and find the top for my castle.

I fasten it up
with the pieces of string
I have saved in my box.

Now my castle is dark.

No one knows I am there.

I look through the side railing

and see the rain bouncing on the sidewalk.

I can see the tops of umbrellas bobbing by.

I can see people

standing under the awning across the street,

waiting for the rain to stop.

They do not see me in my castle.

I am alone in my castle.

I am a king in my castle.

I look at the things in my box.

When the rain has stopped,
there are little puddles in the street.

I go down in my bare feet
and feel the little puddles.

They are very warm.

I walk up and down the street,
feeling all the puddles
until the puddles are dried up.

The sidewalk is hot to my feet.

Then I go back to my castle.

I take down the top of my castle

and fold it and put it away,

the way Mother said.

I see the sky is blue now.

It is almost time for me to see the sun.

I can only see it for a little while every day

when it is just above me.

There it is!

That means it is time for me to have my sandwich.

Mother always puts my sandwich

and my can of juice

on a chair where I can find them.

I eat my sandwich and drink my juice

out in my castle.

I have a bite of sandwich

and then a drink of juice,

until all the sandwich and all the juice are gone.

Then

the sun is behind my building,

and I cannot see it any more.

That means it is time for my nap.

I fix my mattress and pillow.

It is very hot.

I count the railings around the sides of my castle.

One two three, one two three, one two three.

I count the doors across the street.

One two three, one two three, one two three.

My mother says

I am the best counter she has ever known.

I count the windows across the street.

One two three, one two three.

I think I am still counting,

but I have fallen asleep.

I dream that I have found a place to plant my seeds.
It is a big place, as big as my castle.

I dream I plant my seeds, and as soon as I plant a seed
it grows.

First a flower comes, and then a little tree,
and then an apple.

Every day after my nap
I can wish one thing.

Sometimes I wish I could fly.

Sometimes I wish there was always a spider
making webs in my castle, so I could watch.

Sometimes I wish a hundred butterflies would come
to my castle.

They would light on the railing and wave their wings.

Today I wish I had a place to plant my seeds.

I look in my box and count my seeds.
One two three, one two three.

I wonder whether it is time for my mother to come.

I go down to the street.

I go down to the corner

to see if it is time for my mother to come.

I do not cross the street,

but I can see men working from where I am.

It is not time yet. The men are still working

down at the end of the street.

I count my steps. One two three, one two three.

I walk up and down, counting my steps.

Then I count the little lines on the sidewalk.

One two three, one two three.

Now

I stand on the corner again

and see that the men are going away.

They are through working. That means

it is time for my mother to come home.

Now I run.

I run up and down the street.

If I run up and down one two three times,

it will be time for my mother to come.

I go up to my castle and watch for her.

There she comes!
She brings me a bag of jellybeans
and a stick of chewing gum.

She comes out to my castle
and sits with me.

"Pretty soon you will count to ten, pretty baby,"
says my mother.

"Pretty soon you will tell time, pretty baby,"
she says.

I smooth the paper from the chewing gum.
I put the paper in my box.
I show my mother how many seeds I have.

"Seeds can't grow unless they have a place
to be planted," says my mother.

My mother and I have our sandwich,
sitting in my castle. We have a glass of milk.

She tells me more about counting.

"Five, five, five—one two three four five.
One two three four five," she says over and over.

"You're surely the best counter I know,"
says my mother.

It is time for the lights to come on.

It is time for the music to start.

My mother gives me an apple
to save for the morning.

I put it in my box.

My mother says
there are many little lights in the sky—
little stars—maybe a hundred for all she knows.

Some day
she will take me where I can see all of them.

Some day
when I can count to a hundred.

I lie on my stomach.

I look to see whether my friends

Mr. and Mrs. Rodriguez

are in their castle.

They are not.

I look at the bright lights across the street.

I listen to the music and the talking and the laughing.

I have my box beside me.

I count the railings on my castle.

One two three four five, one two three four five,

one two three four five.